Día de mercado

Una historia contada a través del arte popular

Escrita y diseñada por

Lois Ehlert

Traducida por F. Isabel Campoy y Alma Flor Ada

Libros Viajeros • Harcourt, Inc.

San Diego   Nueva York   Londres

Canta el gallo ro[jo] ... [ma]ñanita.

...tense.

...luelos

maíz.

Saca las zanahorias.
Sacude la tierra.
Empaqueta los
tomates.
Arréglate la camisa.

Da de comer al gallo rojo, al pavo y al ganso. Cierra bien la verja para que no se salgan.

Carga el camión.

Estamos listos
para ir...

cruzando los campos donde crecen las

verduras,

pasando a los pájaros en
las ramas,
pasando a las serpientes
que toman el sol
en la brisa,

que nadan cerca del puente,

y pasando a
las ovejas
que pastan
en la sierra.

hasta que el sol
se pone al
final
del día.

Entonces cargamos el camión, y con su triquitraque subimos la sierra,

bajamos la cuesta,
cruzamos el puente,

pasamos los árboles, ruedan de prisa las ruedas, cruzamos los campos.

Por fin estamos en casa.
¡Vamos a comer!

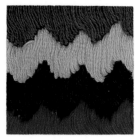

cubierta y contracubierta
origen: Guatemala
materiales: algodón,
hilo de bordar

gallo
origen: Guatemala
materiales: madera,
pintura

serpiente (rayada)
origen: Estados Unidos
materiales: madera, pintura

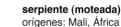

serpiente (moteada)
orígenes: Mali, África
materiales: madera, diseño quemado

tajada de sandía
origen: México
materiales: madera, pintura
(ojos de papel añadidos)

verduras
orígenes: México, Estados Unidos
materiales: papel maché, pintura

pavo
origen: Guatemala
materiales: madera,
pintura

pájaros
origen (el marrón y el anaranjado): África
origen (el rojo): India
origen (el resto): Estados Unidos
materiales: madera, tela, cuentas, metal, pin

pollo
origen: Guatemala
materiales: madera, pintura

camión
origen: México
materiales: barro, pintura

gallina de guinea
origen: África
materiales: madera, pintura

**árbol (detalle de la
granja en apliqué)**
origen: Colombia
materiales: tela, hilo

fruta
orígenes: Méxi
Estados Unido
materiales: pap
maché, pintura

**pollitos
(detalle de la granja en apliqué)**
origen: Colombia
materiales: tela, hilo

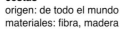

cestas
origen: de todo el mundo
materiales: fibra, madera

libélula
origen: China
materiales:
madera, pintura

personas
origen: México
materiales: barro, pintura

grillo
origen: China
materiales: junco

casa (detalle de la granja en apliqué)
origen: Colombia
materiales: tela, hilo

**ganso
(reclamo de caza)**
origen: Estados Unidos
materiales: metal,
madera, pintura

toro
origen: África
materiales: cuentas, relleno

mariposa
origen: Perú
materiales: fibra
tejida y tintada

mariposa (detalle textil de una mola)
origen: Panamá
materiales: algodón, hilo

moto
origen: África
materiales:
latas de metal
desechadas,
alambre, cadena
de bicicleta,
goma, plástico

pelota
origen: Guatemala
materiales: algodón,
estambre, relleno

muñeca (precolombina)
origen: Perú
materiales: lana, algodón,
agujas de tejer

muñecas en forma de ratones
origen: Indonesia
materiales: algodón, madeja de lana

muñeca (de retazos)
origen: Estados Unidos
materiales: fibra,
algodón

muñeca (con cuentas)
origen: África
materiales: tela,
relleno, semillas,
cuentas

muñeca/cepillo
origen: México
materiales: palma

flores
orígenes: México,
Estados Unidos
materiales: papel crepé,
alambre

...es y ranas
...o de pesca en el hielo)
...: Estados Unidos
...eriales: madera, metal, pintura, ojos de
...llo, cuentas, chinchetas, plomo en la
...ga

oveja (detalle de la granja en apliqué)
origen: Colombia
materiales: tela, hilo

camión
origen: Colombia
materiales: barro, pintura

muñeca/bolso
origen: Bolivia
material: madeja de lana

mercado de verduras
origen: Perú
materiales: algodón,
relleno, hilo de bordar

tíovivo o carrusel
origen: Estados Unidos
materiales: madera,
pintura, tornillos, tuercas

bueyes, carro, carretero
origen: México
materiales: madera, pintura, cuerda

animal (rayado)
origen: México
materiales: madera,
clavos, pintura

corazones
origen: México
materiales: cuentas, algodón

muñeca
origen: México
materiales:
algodón, lana

detalles de tela
origen: Guatemala
materiales: algodón

luna/estrellas
origen: México
materiales: hojalata, pintura

...ndía (la tajada se puede remover)
...en: México
...teriales: madera, pintura

zarigüella
origen: México
materiales: barro, pintura

carro/arreos
origen: Estados Unidos
materiales: fibra,
madera, metal

jaguar
origen: México
materiales: madera, pintura

sol
origen: México
material: hojalata

¿ De dónde
vinieron?
¿ De qué
están hechos?

Para Allyn

www.HarcourtBooks.com

This is a translation of *Market Day: A Story Told with Folk Art*.

First Libros Viajeros edition 2003
Libros Viajeros is a trademark of Harcourt, Inc., registered in the United States of America and/or other jurisdictions.

Library of Congress Cataloging-in-Publication Data
Ehlert, Lois.
[Market Day. Spanish.]
Día de mercado: una historia contada a través del arte popular/escrita y diseñada por Lois Ehlert; traducida por F.
Isabel Campoy y Alma Flor Ada.
p. cm.
"Libros Viajeros."
Summary: On market day, a farm family experiences all the fun and excitement of going to and from the farmers'
market.
[1. Markets—Fiction. 2. Farm life—Fiction. 3. Stories in rhyme. 4. Spanish language materials.]
I. Campoy, F. Isabel. II. Ada, Alma Flor. III. Title.
PZ74.3.E6 2003
[E]—dc21   2001051800
ISBN 0-15-216814-1

H G F E D C B A

The handmade objects photographed to illustrate this book are from Lois Ehlert's collection, with the following
exceptions: the Guatemalan chicken, lent by Allyn Johnston; the Chinese cricket, lent by Pat Ehlert; and the African
spotted snake, lent by Dick Ehlert, who also carved the robin, the striped snake, and the red-winged blackbird.

The author made the following elements in order to complete the compositions: embroidery fragments, corn, carrots,
cauliflower, the harness and cart for the opossum, and the Ferris wheel.

Photographs by John Nienhuis, Lillian Schultz, and Lois Ehlert

The display type and text type were set in Century Expanded.
Color separations by Tien Wah Press Limited, Singapore
Printed and bound by Tien Wah Press, Singapore
Production supervision by Sandra Grebenar and Wendi Taylor

Garfield
hangs out

BY JIM DAVIS

Ballantine Books • New York

PROFESSOR GARFIELD'S
NATURAL HISTORY OF DOGS

PROTO-DOG
A BRAINLESS SLIME DWELLER.

DOGOSAUR 12 MILLION B.C.
HAD THE MISFORTUNE TO LIVE BEFORE TREES AND FIRE HYDRANTS HAD EVOLVED; SOON EXTINCT.

CRO-MAGNON DOG 10,000 B.C.
DOMESTICATED BUT STILL NOT HOUSEBROKEN.

WOOD-BURNING DOG CA. 1850
ANOTHER MISTAKE.

MODERN DOG
AS YOU CAN SEE, NOT A LOT OF PROGRESS.

9

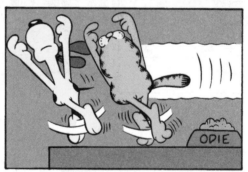

23

GOOD, GARFIELD'S NOT AROUND. I WON'T HAVE TO SHARE MY MILK

MY DATE WAS GOING REAL WELL TONIGHT

MY SOPHISTICATION SWEPT HER OFF HER FEET

THEN I NOTICED I WAS WEARING MY UNDERWEAR ON THE OUTSIDE OF MY PANTS

SICK

GARFIELD, YOU MADE ME BREAKFAST!

WHAT IS IT?

I'LL GIVE YOU A HINT

MMMM...

WHAT HAS SIX LEGS AND CAN'T SWIM IN ORANGE JUICE?

41

59

THE PRIMA BALLERNIA JETÉS ONTO THE STAGE

© 1989 PAWS, INC. All Rights Reserved.

7-9

THE OLYMPIC GYMNAST FINISHES HIS ROUTINE WITH A FULL BACK LAYOUT

HERE WE ARE IN THE FINAL ROUND OF THE HOPSCOTCH COMPETITION

THE JACKHAMMER OPERATOR RIPS THROUGH 12 INCHES OF CONCRETE

OH, GARFIELD

JIM DAVIS

WHY CAN'T YOU JUST NUZZLE LIKE OTHER CATS?

YOU DESERVE BETTER

HEY, GARFIELD! WE'RE GOING TO THE FARM TODAY!

FINE, I'LL BE OUTSIDE...

LETTING THE AIR OUT OF YOUR TIRES

JIM DAVIS 7-10

DOC BOY! HOW ARE YOU?

DON'T CALL ME DOC BOY!

OH, SORRY. HMMM WHAT ELSE DID I USED TO CALL YOU?...

OH, YEAH! IGUANA GUMS! HOW ARE YOU?

CALL ME DOC BOY

JIM DAVIS 7-11

SURE IS PEACEFUL HERE

YUP, ALWAYS HAS BEEN. ALWAYS WILL BE. NOTHING MOVES FAST HERE. NOPE

OH, BOYS! DINNER!

JIM DAVIS 7-12

HOW'S IT GOING?

HAVEN'T QUITE GOT THE HANG OF IT

7-27

WORRIED ABOUT WRINKLES, GARFIELD?

JUST REMEMBER, WRINKLES ONLY EXIST TO SHOW WHERE THE SMILES HAVE BEEN

YOUR LIFE MUST BE A LAUGH RIOT

OH, SHUT UP

7-28

Z

STOMP

ZINNNG!

HE DIDN'T EVEN SAY "GOODBYE"

7-29

69

I'M BEGINNING TO THINK THERE'S A BIGGER WORLD OUT THERE...

A SIXTY-FOURTH OF AN INCH LAST NIGHT, GARFIELD!

CONGRATULATIONS, JON

THOSE TOENAILS ARE REALLY GROWING NOW

JIM DAVIS 7-31

GARFIELD, I CAN'T SCRATCH YOU ANY LONGER. MY HANDS ARE CRAMPING UP

FINE

POOK!

JIM DAVIS 8-1

I LOVE GOURMET COOKING, GARFIELD

IF IT DOESN'T MOVE, I'LL EAT IT

8-2

CREATIVITY IS THE KEY

IF IT MOVES A LITTLE, I'LL EAT IT

I JUST CAN'T GET THE MEAT LOAF INSIDE THE DANISH

HECK WITH IT. IF I CAN CATCH IT, I'LL EAT IT

JIM DAVIS

SIGH... MONDAY

IT'S DREARY, AND POURING RAIN

WHAT COULD BE WORSE?

THERE'S A MOTORCYCLE GANG IN THE DRIVEWAY

JIM DAVIS   9-11

SHOULD I BE MEAN OR LAZY TODAY?...

OR, MAYBE A HAPPY MEDIUM...

I'LL JUST LIE HERE AND BITE ANYONE WHO TRIPS OVER ME

JIM DAVIS   9-12

THIS DAY IS THE DULLEST...

THINGS CAN'T GET MORE BORING THAN THIS...

ANY MORE STAMPS AROUND HERE?

BINGO

JIM DAVIS   9-13

AND NOW A SCIENTIFIC EXPERIMENT TO SEE IF **DOGS** CAN LAND ON THEIR FEET

BLOONG

9-21

I HATE EATING IN BED

THERE MUST BE SOME DEEP PSYCHOLOGICAL REASON FOR THAT...

OR MAYBE IT'S BECAUSE I'M LYING ON MY FORK

9-22

SOMETIMES IT'S GOOD TO GET UP EARLY AND DO CHORES

AARRRGGH!

LIKE MOVING THE LITTER BOX TO THE SIDE OF JON'S BED

9-23